The Book of Conjurations

SUNDIAL HOUSE

The Book of Conjurations

Irizelma Robles Álvarez

Translated by
Roque Raquel Salas Rivera

SUNDIAL HOUSE   NEW YORK   •   PHILADELPHIA

**SUNDIAL
HOUSE**
New York ♦ Philadelphia

Book design: Lisa Hamm

Cover image: Ana Rosa Rivera Marrero

Proofreader: Emily Oliveira

Editorial Assistants: Arianne Morel Flath and
Lizdanelly López Chiclana

ISBN: 979-8-9879264-4-4

Contents

The Book of Conjurations 21

Invoking the City 37

Achemy's Playthings   57

The Evil Eye   95

Introduction

IRIZELMA ROBLES[1]
(1973, HATO REY, PUERTO RICO)

BORN IN 1973 in Hato Rey, Puerto Rico, and living out her early years in Toa Baja with her maternal grandparents and her mother, Irizelma Robles grew up near the Dorado River, in a house with much poetry but few poetry books. Her family's commercial interests eventually led them to relocate in the neighboring municipality of Dorado. While residing there, she studied at various private schools where she became passionately interested in literature and was subsequently nicknamed "la loca" or "crazy girl."

Upon graduating from high school, she continued her studies in the Hispanic Studies Department at the Río Piedras Campus of the University of Puerto Rico (UPRRP). She owes her first poetry publication in part to Mayra Santos Febres, founding member of the literary magazine *La mirilla,*

---

1. Personal interviews with the poet (2021-2022).

in which she published her first poems alongside poets such as José Raúl "Gallego" González, Rolando Guardiola, and Alan Figueroa. She also shared a stage with the legendary Nuyorican poet and performer Pedro Pietri, whose work would inspire her own performances later in life.

During her freshman year, one of her professors mentioned that she had just returned from the National Autonomous University of Mexico (UNAM), sparking Robles's interest in graduate study. In 1995, upon graduating from the UPRRP, she decided to apply to the UNAM and moved to Mexico City, where she lived for the next six years. While living there, she became familiar with the Neo-Baroque poetry of José Carlos Becerra, David Huertas, and Coral Bracho, all of whom had a strong influence on her early work. Her graduate studies were focused on Náhuatl culture and she completed field work in La Huasteca, forging lasting relationships and commitments not only as an investigator and writer, but also as an ethnographer. It was during these years that she met her husband, José Marcial Cortés Ávila, and in 1999 she had a child, Salomé Cortés Robles, who would also go on to become a poet and visual artist.

Her years in Mexico provided Robles with time to continue reading and writing, both contemporary Mexican poetry and the poetry of Puerto Rican writers such as Vanessa Droz and Aurea María Sotomayor, thus sustaining a relationship with her peers and an ever-growing knowledge of Puerto Rico's literary production. Although her writing during this period was not something she shared or published, she absorbed much and grew as a poet thanks to the different cultural scenes she participated in as an avid listener and reader. All of her interactions and experiences later informed her first full-length poetry book, *De pez ida*, which she describes as strongly-shaped by Neo-Baroque tendencies.

After three years raising a child while completing her PhD in Mesoamerican Studies, she earned her degree in 2002 and decided to return to Puerto Rico in the midst of a divorce. Once back on the archipelago, she began teaching as an adjunct professor at various institutions, including the Inter American University of Puerto Rico, the University of Puerto Rico, Center for Advanced Studies of Puerto Rico and the Caribbean.

With a grant from the National Endowment for the Arts, Robles published *De pez ida* (Isla Negra Ediciones, 2003). The book was partially edited by one of her mentors, the poet Joserramón "Ché" Melendes, with whom she met regularly to discuss her poems. By the time she had a complete manuscript, however, it had changed significantly under the influence of Elba Macías, a writer whose imagery shared some characteristics with Neo-Baroque poets. Under Macías's guidance, Robles's style underwent a transformation that began with *De pez ida* and found its final form in the 2008 collection, *Isla mujeres* (Fragmento Imán).

Isla mujeres, her second full-length book, was intentionally a Neo-Baroque exercise that the poet eventually abandoned while writing her third poetry book, *Agave azul* (2015). This third collection was the first she published with Editorial Folium, thus establishing a lasting relationship with editor Eugenio Ballou. She describes it as a return to brief, condensed poems.

Beginning with her return to her homeland and a diagnosis in 2002, Robles had been struggling with Bipolar II disorder and a related series of hospitalizations over a period of thirteen years. These cumulative experiences led her to reflect on the relationship between poetry, subjection, colonialism, social body, gender, and individual experience in the book *El libro de los conjuros* (2018), which I have translated as *The Book of Conjurations*. The writing itself took little time and, in a recent interview, the poet has described it as intense, condensed, and brief, the result of the life-long struggle of being neurodivergent in an ableist world.

Robles continued writing in this minimalist mode throughout her most recent books: *Alumbre* (Editorial del Instituto de Cultura Puertorriqueña, 2018) and *El templo de Samye* (Folium, 2020). Her work has received overdue critical attention and praise in recent years and, in 2021, she won SUNY-Stony Brook's Pedro Lastra First International Poetry Prize for her latest book *Lacustre* (Trabalis Editores, 2021). She currently lives between Puerto Rico and Mexico, where she is working on her spiritual practice, writing poetry, and advocating for an end to mental health stigma in Puerto Rico.

THE BOOK OF CONJURATIONS (FOLIUM, 2018)

According to P.G. Maxwell-Stuart in *The Chemical Choir,* there are primarily two kinds of alchemists: those who sought material wealth and made a living conning kings by promising instant riches and those for whom gold was but a metaphor of transformation and transcendence. In both groups, there were more than a few alchemists who were also poets.[2] Poetry, like alchemy, can promise a material wealth it never quite delivers, transmutation through words, and the power to turn paupers into patrons. Poetry, however, most often promises an alchemy of the soul that strives toward a higher form. Irizelma Robles is best described as the latter form of alchemist and *El libro de los conjuros/The Book of Conjurations*, her fourth poetry collection, transforms poet, reader, and language. Among these pages, we find all forms of material existence transmuted. Barbwire, rain, soul, sugarcane, and scream are all raw materials for alchemy, or poetry.

Drawing from the periodic table, precious and semiprecious stones, minerals, rocks, the elements, flora and fauna

---

2. See, Maxwell-Stuart, P. G. "Introduction," *The Chemical Choir: A History of Alchemy.* London: Bloomsbury Plc, 2012. Pg. ix-xi, Print.

from Puerto Rico, the Caribbean and Latin America, and her memories, Robles creates an alternate cosmogony that neither rejects nor unquestioningly accepts Western medical discourse, yet refrains from advocating for one of many parallel traditions and bodies of knowledge. According to the poet, this is a book "born from [her] need to transform the pain rooted in hospitalizations and [her] experience with depression since [she] was diagnosed with Bipolar II disorder."[3] These poems are written to conjure another life out of this one, a way forward despite and with her neurodivergence, sadness, depression, and anxiety. She imagines herself as the poet-alchemist to conjure another self in that poetic voice, one that not only survived these hospitalizations, but that also found metaphor, images, and poetic motifs in the basest of elements. It is also a voice that found gold to be as useless as it was for all who sought it, a tool of power that ultimately became dead weight in Robles's quest for release.

What makes this alchemy spectacular in its difference is that the elements transform without the poet and before the transmutation. Each element is already living, moving, and changing, so the poetry must work quickly with unstable elements and living matter. In the poem "Marble," she describes

---

3. Personal interview with the poet (February 2022; my translation).

this willingness to work with life as "Malleable, flexible, [...] perfect for the alchemist's foundry, / although neither gold nor clay." It is this malleability that makes Robles the ideal alchemist, one who is more accustomed to failure than to success and for whom alchemy is less about perfection and more about studying the ever-changing nature of that which seemed fixed.

The book's title is itself malleable. "Un conjuro " can be translated as "a spell" or "a conjuration" and this could just have easily been titled *The Spell Book*, but as is suggested in the opening epigraph by the Spanish poet Leopoldo María Panero, "los conjurados" has a different and equally important connotation. To be conjured, to be invoked into a conspiracy, and to be called from the spirit world into this one, all overlap or coincide. Thus, though often used interchangeably with "spell," a conjuration is a specific kind of spell that calls forth something from nothing. Because these are conjurations, they are also a specific kind of alchemy that deals with the spiritual, the crossing over of worlds, and the forging of life through language.

These poems were written after Robles's fifth hospitalization and they bear the traces of years of struggle and a search for life in an openly hostile world. She manages to code personal and painful details of state violence, medical intervention, and institutionalization within these brief and searing poems. When discussing the work, she expressed that she has "never been more vocal about [her] illness, but every-thing has been filtered through the poetic image, metaphor, and other forms of figurative language." The poet feels that she accomplished her aim and managed to say that this ill-ness hurts, thereby reaching others who are similarly suf-fering.[4] But these poems do much more than "say" or even "describe" they transfix and then suddenly transfigure. They design a system structured by movement, the sensorial, intu-ition, trial and error, and, yes, magic.

In the poem "Sand," Robles writes, "I come from the sea, / I have never abandoned / the white fish of the page." The "white fish of the page" comes from that larger body of water; the poem comes from that liquid that knows no borders between self, poem, and reader. Still, other poems in the collection belie a struggle in which alchemy is ultimately failure, the inability to find the right formula or words to transform. The poem "Coal," for example, points to the force-ful selection of the word "sadness" to describe the speaker's experience, thus making something legible for which there are still no words. Robles writes "I walked within the room's four walls. / I forcefully wrote / *sadness* / and they let me go."

---

4. "Nunca he sido más vocal acerca de mi enfermedad pero todo pasado a través de la imagen poética, y la metáfora, entre otras figuras del lenguaje. Al final siento que lo logré, que logré decir que esta enfermedad duele y llegar así a otras personas que también sufren por lo mismo."

Here, I imagine a king, anxious for a remedy, and an alchemist who turns in incomplete formulas in order to buy more time.

The alchemist's signs change. What is wrong for one formula is perfect for another. Where before the word "sadness" is a forced self-diagnosis, in the poem "Prozac" it becomes a shared sorrow. Now, the alchemist has enemies, other alchemists who are "illusionists of joy":

> They force me
> to take a long trip
> to happiness.
> I defend my sadness
> from the wizards of chemistry,
> the illusionists of joy.
> They don't know I store
> tears for future generations,
> placing sorrow in a hidden drawer.

These poems challenge an alchemy that presents itself as the science of diagnosis, an unquestioning altar to reason. In "Cobalt Blue," medical discourse is associated with a long history of conquest, the erasure of previous forms of knowledge, and the possibility that the things designated as illnesses are often other modes of existence:

The doctor takes her by the hand
leading her to an isolated
chair where he will speak to her
of the new world of a diagnosis.

But she is just another number in this bitter cosmos
and her screams rumble like cobalt blue.

This "new world" of the diagnosis, like the "new world" of
the Americas, discovered by Europe, is only new to those who
have not been living there. The act of naming, with its long
colonial history in the form of taxonomy, here becomes diag-
nosis. Robles expresses ambivalence when faced with the fac-
ile solution of the new name, the pill, and the institution. She
questions these structures without outright rejecting all the
experiences they encompass.

The book's two final poems bring this idea home. They
converse openly with Julia de Burgos's late life experiences
as a patient at Harlem Hospital and Goldwater Memorial
Hospital on Welfare Island. "With You at Goldwater Hos-
pital" refers to the way in which De Burgos became com-
pletely invisible as a patient in institutions that did not care
about her poetry and saw, in her status as a recently migrated
Puerto Rican, just another brown body subject to experimen-
tation. Here, "the wind" is the element that transforms and
joins both poets:

the wind carried us
to the shore of a world
without mirrors
where you could be seen,
but you were indelible,
pure ink.

The ending suggests that De Burgos became "pure ink" through her death and before she could be fully "seen," but the word "shore" leaves us with an unresolved ambiguity. Does that shore belong to Puerto Rico or Welfare Island? If the latter, is visibility then a liability, a threat, depending on the beholder?

The book's final poem is more subtle in its allusion to De Burgos; perhaps, more coded. "176058" refers to the infamous moment when De Burgos wrote "poet" as her profession on a form and the staff crossed it out and wrote "patient suffers from delusions." The impossibility of poetry as alchemy and poet as world maker finds its final form in this tragicomic moment in which De Burgos's reality is read as a delusional impossibility.

Alchemy itself is popularly viewed as an outdated pseudo-science, surpassed by scientific reason.[5] It is no coincidence

---

5. See P.G. Maxwell-Stuart. "Introduction," *The Chemical Choir: A History of Alchemy*. London: Bloomsbury Plc, 2012. ix–xi.

then that Robles finds common ground with De Burgos, the woman who wrote the poem "Nada" or "Nothingness" in response to early twentieth-century materialist existentialism and as a celebration of embodied pleasure. Beyond the logic of institutions and the discourses of modernity, both seek in poetry the creative potential that makes something from nothing and that takes devalued lives and imbues them with supernatural qualities.

Translating Irizelma Robles's *El libro de los conjuros* and transmuting it into *The Book of Conjurations* has been one of the most satisfying translation projects I have undertaken in the last few years. The resonances, cadences, allusions, images, and outright beauty in these poems are only surpassed by Irizelma herself, my friend and a poet I admire, who took the time to sit with me and discuss these translations. Time and time again, throughout our conversations since we became friends, we have come back to the subject of mental illness, its history, pathologies, neurodivergence, and poetry. Both of us seem to have found our languages in poems, whose counterspells and conjurations have helped us survive, even thrive, our own minds. I can only hope to have done her words justice with these translations and to share her fire with new readers.

It was raining and, after the sunset was followed by the night of the conjured, the world was no longer anything more than cadavers and rain and the voices of old women speaking in the shadows.

Leopoldo María Panero

To my mother

The Book of Conjurations

Alchemista

For Elizabeth Magaly Robles

DANZAR

You write *danzar*
on the cloth
and we dance together
ancient priests
about to spray
saliva and semen
on bare-boned faces.

TRANSPARENCY

A lit wick
melts the tapestries.

The wax slides
to uncover pain
and break the wound.

A lock of your hair
rests on this transparency.

THE SILENCE OF THE HOURS

You change something of yours into ours:
suns, tapestries, wax monsters.

Something of ours stays in you
marking the silence of the hours

THEIR NAME

Out of the fabric
rises a world of newborn,
and never before objects.

Now they exist
and their name is indelible.

CHIAROSCURO

You are only shielded
by the intention and certainty
that the street
is chiaroscuro.

The world interrupted
for a brief moment
blooms.

UNWAXED

A bright wax light
sleep is unlit by the fire's
stunning bite. [1]

Unwaxed
she sees, her agony now apparent.

---

1. I have translated the rhyme of "encendida" and "mordida" in Spanish into "light" and "bite."

WAXGALL

Your hands above wax:
creatures of waxgall
for cutting shade.

Immense animals
skip along corridors.

THE INCONCLUSIVE

You trace its shape:
medusas, amoebas,
silhouettes of something perishable,
sketches for the inconclusive.

SEAMLESS PLOT

Wax animals
of fiber and tendons
that reach life
caught in your weaver hands.

Embracing the stripped flesh of fabric
they survive in their bodies'
seamless plot.

ON WAX

I imagine an unlit wick
that over*lacerates* your fingers.

If I were to light it,
they'd die with one strike, those
ferocious animals of linen and honey.

THE POEM

The fabrics
stand up,
threatening to skip and jump
under the intense rain
of a mysterious sadness.

The Book of Conjurations

BIRDS, FLOWERS, AND SYMBOLS

Decanting metals
I'll forge into birds,
flowers, and symbols.

Scandium and chromium
transmuted into signs
will speak the truth of things.

I'll listen attentively for such is the world.

THE POTTER'S WHEEL

Musk
for shaping the figure out of gold
that will shine on my fingers
like clay on a potter's wheel.

Language
will say inconclusive things
so that I must finish phrases.

New being born of unbaked clay.

GOLD AND CLAY

Gold and clay
rise from my dream.

Batches of this new substance
now feed
the childhood illusions
of alchemists.

If they add flowers or sugar
to my reverie's
incandescent mixture:
silver, copper, or tin.

THE MYSTERY OF FLOWERS

Tonight, I discover
the mystery of flowers.
I conjure
and reach the other shore
where they rest peacefully
in their illuminated pond.

MINERAL FISH

Faint like the wandering aroma of andesite,
subtle like wind impregnated
with the scent of gold and serpent.
Good and bad air
that awakens the senses,
that which flees and returns,
the mineral life of a fish
ethereal as spume.

INK AND CAMPHOR

Ink and Camphor
bloom in
The Book of Conjurations
under the skiesrosy
of this opaque and silent room
where a flame is the only possible sun.

The humidity of ink
lends its breath
to white pages
where not a single word
spells out the path.

Only the science of the elements remains
and the healing scent of camphor

CONJURATION OF THE DAY

I sing and evaporate water
that contains various elements
for magic and transmutation.

Eucalyptus, rosemary, sap,
the names I can't recognize
on the faces that stare,
pieces of language
erased like mist.

All shines a slow light
on unborn things.

I try to memorize the conjuration
in a superhuman effort
refusing to change the one I love
into an unknown animal.

ALCHEMIST OF THE TETRAVALENT POEM

for Gaston Bachelard

Alien to my dreams,
he has lent me his own:
land and fantasies of repose,
air and dreams,
the psychoanalysis of fire,
the skin of the poem,
water and dreams,
his bonfire.

THE ELEMENTS

In my fantasy
water will make way for the earth
that will listen
as I conjure collapse,
the landslide
of air between my fingers.

CONJURATION FOR LIES

The Supreme Alchemist
conjures in order to silence
lies and suspicions,
whoever listens
will only speak the truth
even if love
has set sail.

PREDICTION

To bestow on the beloved
the capacity for loving,
this is faith,
the only thing left
for us to divine.

TO ALLOY, TO ASCEND

To alloy,
softening the metals
until they are dust.
To see life surge
from their death
because they will rise
like the quetzal bird,
from nothing, in the purest silence.

To alloy, to ascend
on metal wings
until reaching the roof,
invading it with feathers.

Birds of prey
clean the bones of deceit and misfortune.

THE BOOK OF CONJURATIONS

It opens its pages
for anyone who
imitates the songs of birds.
Closing them
on whomever fears
or trembles.

Invoking the City

TO CROSS

the avenue awaits me
I could throw myself
onto the empty road
reaching the other shore
outlining my feet on the bird
that arrives
with its noisy
trucks,
ambulances,
and cop cars
I could cross

DRIZZLE

Drizzle keeps
flooding the barely
traversable road
we learn to jump over
puddles of dirty water
with city verve
and we unwittingly
play hopscotch

STREETLIGHTS

maddening reds
spokespeople for hatred
and living on standby
iniquities of silence

cars stop

for a moment
stop beating

until the city's eyes
change color

STREETS

Valencia Street
Cerra Street
Monserrate Street
petite streets
and alleyways
speak the truth
about their houses
and walls
daubed
with letters and symbols
understood only by
vagabonds
and their dogs

OPALESCENT

the rain
those shards
belong to the ground

it rains
and its descendancy is transformed
iridescent

I feel a light humidity
and collapse into a thatched armchair
I've reserved for
days like today

MURAL

graffiti writes the city
inscribes us in its landscape
ephemeral like its corners
urbs and orbs
sunflowers
turn right
and to the left
on its skin we see the lasting mark
of the raw paintbrush
the dense moon

HOUSES

Evening serpents
slither with their
illuminated skin
when the smell of gasoline
disappears and the garden
survives the smog
thus reaching nocturnal freedom
the next day
they are gone

TWO STREETS DOWN

two streets down
I find peace
in the café
others like me
prefer to forget
their sorrows in cupsful
of daily consumption
that no longer improves
with the clean air of the countryside

THE REVOLVING DOOR

for Pedro Pietri

I don't know your labyrinths
your streets unnarratable
the time that you trailed
on your way to
the revolving door
you left me your signature
scribbled in a book
upon seeing your handwriting
jumping out from the page
I recognize your laughter

TWO STREETS UP

the sound of construction
equipment
drowns out the voices of workers
going to lunch at ten
if I could hear them
I'd learn the language
of the streets

HOSPITALS

the nurse
in the tidy uniform
gives us a small glass of water
we use to rush the pill down
and a commiserating smile
which we barely thank
while the white coats
make waves in hallways

temperature, pulse, pressure
all indicate we are still alive

THE APT.

I discover my solitude
in a one-room
apartment
with a gas stove
and a bathroom small
enough
for surviving
absence
and the presence
of the only couch

RIGHT TURN

I turn right
when I reach my bed
I turn when exposed
to my own weather
I crawl under
the sheet's folds
in my creases
I discover the nightmare
of waking up to yesterday

TURN LEFT

I turn left
I walk the path
in silence until
I reach the park
I sit down
and myself feel
time and darkness
merge
with the bench
where I calmly take my rest

SANTURCE

for Noemí Segarra

I live in the City
where we barely fit
and sorrows harden
like sidewalks
as we traverse them
like ants
I roam its streets
on foot or await the bus
a meeting place
for the main
characters
in the city storyline
I step on the hard concrete
of Santurce
I let it speak to me
in its garbled
language

RODENTS

pets of the human city
that circles
and gnaws away at us
I imagine them beneath my feet
in the urban underworld
confined to night

THE VAGABOND AND HIS DOG

I've thought that some day
I'll stop passing the street
where he has made a home

that soon I'll stop seeing
his dog on the facing
sidewalk
waiting for the whistle
that will get him to cross
with confidence

I've wanted to leave
something of myself to that
wound in the scenery

Alchemy's Playthings

ALLOY

On one of its pages
alchemy becomes
an animal that lunges against
the mineral poverty of that instant.

On another page
the animal stares back.

RARE EARTHS

I wander
treading metals
as if crossing burning coals.

Rusty land where
evil elements flourish,
a menacing sky,
the storm.

It slashes and burns.
Only this sadness grows
and this boulder in the road.

FIRE AGATE

I pulverize its hues to call the wind
and banish tears.
Fire ore,
in its silky skin the ardent call lies dormant.
What doesn't wait is the skin
aggregate of agate and amber.
The venomous transformation,
the torment.

ADULARIA

I feel
its sorrows and fears
in the pained texture
of its surface.

Might there be pigeons
and lintels
within?

BRECCIA

Breaking through the rubble[2]
of a sealed sorrow,
there is no air
and life hides
to cry in shame.

Pain hardens me.

A rocky mass
formed by that intensity
alters the size of rocks.

---

2. "Brecha" in Spanish makes reference both to the rock and to the expression "romper brecha" ("bridge the gap"). I have used "Breccia" and "rubble" since it comes from the Italian word for rubble. Rather than bridge the gap, I imagined the breaking down of a wall and the subsequent breaking through the rubble to make room for air.

ANDESITE

Volcanic remains,
stone that treads on stone,
nobody that treads on nothing.
I've just been born from the eruption.
Andesite, only the smoke gives me away,
only the ash is content.

AQUA AURA

Crystalline, pure,
cobalt petal,
harmony of nets,
flying fish
with a blue aura.

Do I dream on time or
dream ill-timed?

A voice echoes,
it is the water that imbibes its crystals,
which I carry around my neck
for beautification.

SANDSTONE

A pinch
is enough for scribes
to dye the surface of signs
and symbols not deciphered.

Sandstone,
double stone of quartz and sand,
leaves its words of love with mine.

BASALT

I invoke the gods of basalt,
I ask for a renewed life,
full of life.
In return I receive alabaster,
granite,
volcanic rock,
magma.

IRON

The green, plastic bed.
The prison, the restrictions, the hallway,
to write only with a pencil,
barred from hurting oneself even within.
Drowning and numbness,
it's impossible to thread the details,
to spin stories.
In this cemetery
Lezama is a fragment,
iron fillings,
a magnet.

LEAD

Self-leadened
I don't rest
nor think of dawn.
I stop looking at the sky
scanning for news of the birds
and it is not hard to discern
heaviness from lightness,
black from white,
the absolutely gray.

MARBLE

Malleable, flexible, it's perfect for the alchemist's
foundry, although neither gold nor clay
will rise from this immobile body.
At most dry flowers, faded violets,
sandstone, flimsy sculptures,
uninhabitable houses.

LAPIS LAZULI

You pencil-draw, a lápiz,[3] your ultramarine blue.
From the other side of the sea,
the beyond, who dwells?

Then I recognize me.

I glimpse my eyes and my skin
on that side, blue-blue and
so intense.

---

3. Playing on both the English and Spanish ways to read "a lápiz": "pencil-drawn" in Spanish and "a pencil" or a "lapis lazuli stone" in English.

CALCITE

White or blue,
either way transparent.
Through its translucence shines what is sky on earth,
what is cloud in wave,
what I carry of myself toward others,
the little girl that is my shadow,
the mineral essence of my tenderness.
Calcite is nourishment
for the immensity of time
and my dead hours.[4]

---

4. In Spanish can be "dead hours" or "spare time."

TANTALUM

The acidity of my tears,
their crystalline heaviness,
undeniable,
miniature rivers.

To flood, to refuse,
to resist corrosion,
to remain intact above time.

My face is time already past,
future time that will pass.

Hard as tantalum,
it resists.

SWEET BARBWIRE

Sweet copper barbwire,
happy alloy of sugarcane and gold,
I come covered in scales,
a new ore
that will swim through
the clay pond toward its death.

SAND

for my siblings
Chiquita and Papal

I come from the sea,
I have never abandoned
the white fish of the page.
I am one step away from burying
my body and covering it in seaweed.
That silent game
between siblings is the memory
of a happy childhood.
The memory or the promise
of a life unearthed.

COAL

Since when do I exist?
For thousands of years, I have dreamt
of being another. A radiocarbon test
dates back to the year 1524.
On that date I arrived on unknown lands
to write in the Nahuatl language
motolinía, motolinía,
she who is poor and sad.
Barefoot and exiled
I walked within the room's four walls.
I forcefully wrote
sadness
and they let me go.

MERCURY

I sleep for entire days
in a quicksilver sea.
Mercurial,
I imitate the bear's hibernation,
I must avoid the implacable cold
of that impoverished love.
I dream for entire days
of a new house
and two children.
I'm afraid to wake up
and I stay asleep.
Neither linden tea
nor the naranjo leaves
resurrect me.
I die at a slow rate,
day after day,
paying others no mind.

OPIATE

Oxidized thirst
to heal the pain,
pill
after pill
to cover up the natural
state of things.
She was no longer my grandmother,
but rather that woman
somewhere between asleep and awake
that loved me,
I know this,
even in her silence.

LITHIUM

Oxygenated water,
expandable Band-Aid
for the emotions,
pure alcohol,
disinfectant for old wounds
and bitter tricks,
fierce pliers against spite.

PROZAC

for Mayda Colón[5]

They force me
to take a long trip
to happiness.
I defend my sadness
from the wizards of chemistry,
the illusionists of joy.
They don't know I store
tears for future generations,
placing sorrow in a hidden drawer.

---

5. See Mayda Colón, *Prosac*, self-published in 2013.

BOHRIUM

No one can face me.

I drag along whoever looks
into the center of my scream
only to scream louder.

My boreal scream,
ambiguous element,
an ancient metal in transit,
a sea that crosses the barriers
of silence.

COBALT BLUE

Of all the nameless women
there is one who keeps crying until she drowns,
screaming that she wants to leave the world and life,
that no one can save her.

The doctor takes her by the hand
leading her to an isolated
chair where he will speak to her
of the new world of a diagnosis.

But she is just another number in this bitter cosmos
and her screams rumble like cobalt blue.

AQUAMARINE

When we hear
the nine o'clock call
no one wants to expose
their eagerness to
fly right over pain,
the burden of routine,
the shaking of arms
nor come out to drink
the blue,
the relief,
the brief moment.

TIN

I miss those days
when I was happy
just remembering my child
drawing pictures in the air
or building sand castles.
But I left them hungry
and did not open my eyes to see.
Just as tin
gives way to bronze,
that youngest
and despicable son,
I abandoned matters of the soul
and, finally,
life.

THALLIUM

for Milagros

I remember the sound of the shot.
My aunt took me running
to the bed where she lay,
the unknown body
of a nameless woman.
The blood drowned everything.

Back at the house
I played *a la víbora de la mar* with my cousins
but I never played hide-and-seek again.

Stems of silence wrapped me
flowerless, leafless.

Thallium discolored
upon touching the air.

OBSIDIAN

Sharp ancient knife,
the remains of cold lava
like the perennial night
that pierces me with its blade.

I learn to die again
run through by the shiny black
glass of obsidian.

CADMIUM

Anguish levels
flourish within vital organs
until they are deformed.

Alchemy's plaything,
the witch makes a fatal cut
on the ductile surface
which, in the hands of an innocent girl,
becomes an expired promise, a useless wait.

Love does not give pause or offer truce,
it is war with a deadly weapon,
that remains undiluted, despite intravenous drip or pills,
in the blood made blueish-white as cadmium.

AMBER

for Migdalia Umpierre

That smell clings to my memory
with a tenacious, unblinking force.
Amber is dragonfly flower,
a spider and ant aquarium,
amber pain that comes to life
if it carries inside the fossil of
a defeated butterfly-heart.

ETHER

Ethyl taste, the scent of dreams
coiled to my desire:
I just want to sleep

Ethereal journey
towards a new inevitable
awakening.

Sad and aged
they confuse me with the stars.

There is no light that can reverberate
in the sterile vigil
of this unfulfilled wish.

SUNFLOWER OPAL

I bloom toward the ore
intent on
separating its essence
and transforming its opacity
into flower salts.
The opal resists
with intense will,
a millenary sunflower stone.

SCANDIUM

If I go back to being six,
if I see myself playing alone
between excessively white walls,
street noises
and a defeated mother
playing alone at losing,
it is to seek myself
in that sad doll
I threw into the void
along with past words
and the toys I shared with no one.

OCEAN JASPER

The hard bark of these fish
knocks against opaque glass,
the mirror's pure and crystalline salt.
They call it *Peje stone*, the fishermen
of this jasper ocean.
Inside this siliceous rock,
these marble veins,
within me, a fish is born,
firstborn sea peje.
It's impossible to swim here,
in the silica, the sylph, the silence.

BLUE SHALE

The day has arrived
and I can feel the
metamorphosis of love into hate.

Someone screams in my ear
that everything is in danger,
that nothing will be saved.

I walk barefoot
across the blue surface of shale.

Nothing stops me,
not screams, not fear.

OPIUM

The hands of a princess
carry me to the bed of smoke
and I rest until dawn.
I wake up recovered and fertile,
ready for love and songs
the beloved sends in sealed envelopes,
　　impossible to open or sing
until the night gives me opium
and everything moves me
to sleep.

The Evil Eye

JET

As a child I wore that little
jet-black hand hanging
from my gold bracelet.

Who could harm me
at such a tender age?

The evil eye came later.

It surprises me
that my mother did not see it coming.

VOLCANIC ROCK

After a long session
and several days of anxiolytics,
she returned as
a teddy bear
turned inside out,
with fuzz on her face
and padded hands.

But time passed
and the screams expelled
magma and ash.

THE UNSPEAKABLE

The desire to live
is reborn and dies,
two instants meet.
Something like
memory and children,
the world and things.
Chrome, that possible word
that shines like silver,
can speak the unspeakable
without breaking.

THE INNER ANIMAL

For some time now
my confinement has lost all importance.

An animal of habit,
I can play in this closet
of irrepressible screams.

I am limestone.

Madness
accompanies us daily,
leaves its imprint stamped
on my body
and its metamorphosis.

We line up again
for breakfast,
lunch,
and dinner.

We live hoping that
the inner animal
will come to the surface
and the rock will grow used to the groan.

REFLECTION

Quicksilver birds
become my mirror.
What they reflect
does not remember man
nor woman.

LOTUS FLOWER

I sit in a lotus position to flee tears and enter
the path. A young girl sits next to me. We take deep
breaths, forgetting the unhappy day that brought us to
this room with green, insufferable walls. Upon arriving,
she was asleep and I came in crying, screaming, about
to suffocate, drowned. But we sat in the lotus position,
half-alive, asked for redemption with one syllable and
left the past behind with its bad promises.

MOTHER, CHILD

My destiny was not traced,
instead left traces of pain
in the corners,
branches of thorns,
the essence of panic.

I picked it up from the floor
and died again
in a vain attempt to
sweep it all and throw it away.

But you turned thirteen
and I wasn't there.

Fate stopped time
when that woman
threatened I'd lose you.

I released my madness
and time spun again
like your thirteen years
and my absence.

WITH YOU AT GOLDWATER HOSPITAL

for Julia de Burgos

When it was not too late
to redeem your name
and my name
the wave separated us,
the wind carried us
to the shore of a world
without mirrors
where you could be seen,
but you were indelible,
pure ink.

176058

Give me my number
And on my wrist
was tattooed
the account
176058
belonging to room 1
in Pavía hospital.

I had already been assigned
my death number[6]
and no one would call me a poet.

---

6. The poet is playing with the expression "número de la suerte" or "lucky number," which here becomes "número de la muerte" or "death number."

IRIZELMA ROBLES was born in Puerto Rico in 1973. She is a poet and essayist who has published the collections of poems *De Pez Ida* (2003), *Isla Mujeres* (2008), *Agave Azul* (2015), *Alumbre* (2018), *El libro de los conjuros* (2018), *El templo de Samye* (2020), *Lacustre* (2020), winner of the International Poetry Award "*Pedro Lastra*," and the anthropology monograph *The Tide of the Dead* (2009).

ROQUE RAQUEL SALAS RIVERA (he/they) is a Puerto Rican poet and translator of trans experience born in Mayagüez, Puerto Rico. His honors include being named Poet Laureate of Philadelphia, the Premio Nuevas Voces, and the inaugural Ambroggio Prize. Among his six poetry books are *lo terciario/ the tertiary* (Noemi Press, 2019), longlisted for the National Book Award and winner of the Lambda Literary Award, and *while they sleep (under the bed is another country)* (Birds LLC, 2019), which inspired the title for *no existe un mundo poshuracán: Puerto Rican Art in the Wake of Hurricane Maria* at the Whitney Museum of American Art. Roque Raquel Salas Rivera has edited the anthologies *Puerto Rico en mi corazón* (Anomalous Press, 2019) and *La piel del arrecife. Antología de poesía trans puertorriqueña* (La Impresora & Atarraya Cartonera, 2023).